Grandpa's
Night Before
Christmas

Sue Carabine

Illustrations by
Shauna Mooney Kawasaki

GIBBS·SMITH
P
PUBLISHER

SALT LAKE CITY

04 03 02 01 00 99   6 5 4 3 2 1

Copyright © 1999 by Gibbs Smith, Publisher

All rights reserved.

Book designed and produced by
Mary Ellen Thompson, TTA Design
Printed and bound in Hong Kong

Published by
Gibbs Smith, Publisher
P.O. Box 667
Layton, Utah 84041

Orders: (1-800) 748-5439
E-mail: info@gibbs-smith.com
Website: www.gibbs-smith.com

ISBN 0-87905-927-3

'Twas the night before Christmas
and Grandpa looked sad,
He couldn't quite fathom
why he felt so bad.

Festivities around him,
Christmas was nigh,
But dear old Grandpa
just heaved a great sigh.

Grandma was baking,
as busy as ever,
Should he go in the kitchen
and bother her? Never!

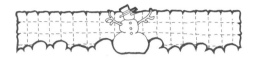

The family was coming,
she had to prepare;
To confide in her now—well,
it wouldn't be fair.

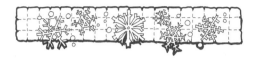

Thoughts of the past
drifted through Grandpa's head,
Seems just like yesterday
he was out in the shed

Splitting logs for the fire
and fixing up lights,
Looking forward so much to
the "Night of all Nights."

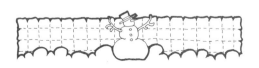

Why, in Christmases past
he'd played a great part,
The season's sweet spirit
had been deep in his heart.

He'd helped his whole family
prepare for the day,
Now it just seemed like
he got in the way!

The shopping was done
and the house was all trimmed,
And Grandpa made sure
that the lights were all dimmed.

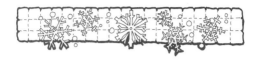

He decided that nothing
could change his sad mood,
Not even the aroma
of wonderful food!

If his family didn't need him
—well, that was okay.
He'd be there with his checkbook
and all bills he'd pay.

He had to get used
to the fact he'd grown old,
And even at Christmas
he would do as he's told!

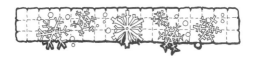

Now somehow the thoughts
of dear Grandpa were heard
By St. Nicholas, who knew
they were really absurd.

Why, the kindness of grandpas
was known far and wide,
And their love for their families
was felt deep inside.

So Santa Claus planted
a thought in the heart
Of each family member,
to play a small part

To make Grandpa feel good
and especially worthwhile,
And also to bring
to his dear face a smile.

The first one to pick up on
St. Nick's super plan
Was Grandma, who felt it
and virtually ran

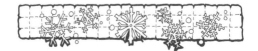

Right into the room
where her dear husband sat,
And promptly she plopped
herself down on his lap.

"Hello, my sweet husband,"
she said with a smile,
"I hope you don't mind
if I sit for a while.

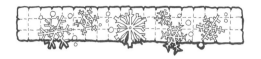

"I missed you while standing
there grating the cheese,"
And Grandpa just grinned
as he gave her a squeeze!

They sat for a while
for no obvious reason,
Just enjoying the sweet
atmosphere of the season.

The Christmas tree lights
and the candles were bliss
And on Grandpa's cheek
Grandma planted a kiss!

All of a sudden they
heard a loud noise—
There were squeals of delight
from glad girls and boys.

The grandkids arrived
and were running full pelt
To the arms of their grandpa,
grabbing onto his belt!

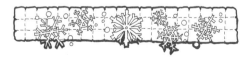

"Hi, Grandma! Hi, Grandpa!"
they yelled with such glee,
And everyone climbed upon
Grandpa's strong knee.

"Thank you for coming
and fixing our sled,
And for painting it, too;
it's an awesome bright red!"

Their mom and their dad
gave Grandpa hugs, too,
"Without you, dear Grandpa,
what on earth would we do?"

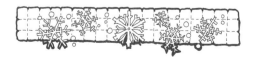

"Our Christmas depended
on getting things done
And when Bessie broke down—
well, it wasn't much fun!

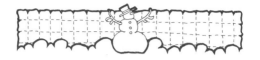

"But you just came right over
as soon as you heard,
And got that car running
without saying a word.

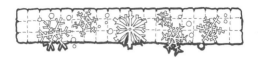

"Now everything's done
and we all made it through.
Oh, Grandpa, our Christmas
is perfect—thank you!"

Not only his family
responded that eve,
But the telephone rang
before they could leave.

"This call is for you, Grandpa.
Hurry, come quick!"
Said sweet little Annie,
"It's your old neighbor Dick."

"Merry Christmas there, Dick,"
Grandpa chuckled aloud,
"Why don't you come over
and join in the crowd?"

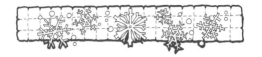

"Thank you, but no,"
Dick said to his friend,
"I'm calling to tell you
I'm grateful no end.

"If you hadn't come over
and shoveled my snow,
There is no way at all
I'd be able to go

"To visit my Martha
who is sitting alone,
Waiting for me
in the town nursing home.

"You are such a fine friend.
I will never forget
Your kindness to me.
Have the best Christmas yet!"

Grandpa thought hard
as he hung up the phone,
Glad that Dick was with Martha
and she wasn't alone.

Just then a loud rapping
was heard at the door.
There stood a young woman
with her children, all four.

"We're here to find Santa,"
Stevie said with such glee,
"I want to thank him
for visiting me.

"Our house is sometimes
so hard to find,
But this year he came
and was ever so kind.

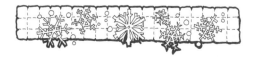

"He brought us a tree
and a basket of food,
Is he here? Have you seen him?
Isn't he good?"

The young single mother
gave Grandpa a glance.
She said softly, "Please tell him,
if you see him by chance,

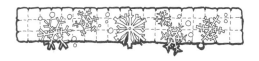

"That we're all very grateful
and we want him to know
That we'll never forget
the great kindness he's shown."

A tear trickled down
Grandpa's face 'cause he knew
That his blessings were many
—he was wrong to feel blue—

With his family around him,
his home full of laughter,
And Christmas cheer ringing
from every rafter.

Santa was touched
when he saw what occurred,
The expressions of caring
and love that he heard.

And a message to grandpas
he desired to give
After seeing the wonderful
way that they lived.

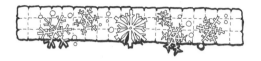

His voice rang out loud
so all grandpas could hear:
"Thank you, my friends,
may your loved ones draw near.

"I wish you could join
in my wondrous flight,
But Merry Christmas, dear grandpas,
to all a Good Night!"